Changing Fortunes

Changing

Fortunes

a collection of short

stories

Kathy Stewart

Changing Fortunes:

a collection of short stories

Copyright © Kathy Stewart 2016

First published in 2016 by

Authors' Ally

www.authorsally.net

27 Wallaby Drive

Mudgeeraba, Qld, 4213

Australia

Stewart, Kathy

Changing Fortunes: a collection of short stories

ISBN: 978-0-9945396-1-8

1st ed.

For Pat and Shelagh, with love

Contents

An African Childhood

The Boer War raged to the north and Mafeking, besieged by the Boers, had just been relieved by the British troops when I came into the world, a mewling, unconcerned infant, the second of two children born to Martha and Albert Moss. The place was East London, situated on the seaboard of the Cape Colony that belonged to the British at that time. Not that I remember much of the city, though we spent my first five years there. My memories of those times are scattered, fragmentary and frozen in time, like images in a kaleidoscope.

We lived in a house far above the harbour, with a view out over the sea that stretched like a giant canvas before us. Ships came and went through the harbour entrance, towed by busy tugs that harried and herded, worrying the bigger vessels to a safe mooring inside the bar. The road to the harbour was a narrow ribbon snaking down to the wharves via dense black-green indigenous bush.

My brother Fred was my leader, my hero. We fashioned rough plank guns and played Boers and British in the front garden, sheltering behind the low garden wall.

Our house was modest, but welcoming, with white painted walls and a rusty iron roof.

Father worked at the carriage makers, persuading hoops of flat iron into wheels. He came home smelling of burnt sawdust, a smell that lingered long after he'd collapsed into his chair beside the stove. That, and the scent of lavender, became the scent of Father and Mother respectively. The scent of our happy times, when we laughed a lot and life was good.

Then Grandpa died.

My last memory of him is seared into my mind, although he lived far away, in the Transkei, at the trading store he'd owned since he was a young man.

Before Grandpa died, he spent some weeks in East London, staying with us for one day – until he went into hospital. The day after he arrived, before Mother realised he was ill, we went on a long trek to show Grandpa the sights.

'The jaunt will do you good, Papa,' she said as he sat at the table, clutching a cup of tea in bony hands. 'I know how much you love walking and nature. You work too hard; you've become quite gaunt.'

We set off early and Father hailed a horse-drawn cab to take us down to the beach front. Grandpa's gaze was unnaturally bright, with water brimming in the corners of each eye every time he coughed.

The cab took us down the hill. Houses clustered along the top of the ridge above the sea line. The pier that separated the river mouth from the beach and formed the head of the harbour stretched out to the right. Fishermen faced the easterlies that blew in from the sea, spraying them with fine salt spray and the scent of seaweed. The esplanade stretched away to the left, past a hotel and some shacks crowding onto a grassy mound.

We alighted at the far end of the esplanade. Father helped Grandpa down and lifted me in his strong arms before depositing me on the ground. Fred clambered down to stand beside Grandpa. Mother held her parasol high above her head, her long skirt brushing the paving, greeting the ladies who promenaded along the seashore.

It was low tide, exposing the rocks and the path that led to Nahoon. We set off along the steep rocky path that linked the two beaches, stopping to watch the waves crash in under the long slabs of rock and spray high into the air through the blow holes they'd created. Red-billed oyster catchers darted across the rocks, their black feathers glistening iridescent green in the sunlight beating down on us.

Fred ran ahead, stopping now and again to check on us struggling along the path behind him.

Grandpa collapsed onto the sand when we reached Nahoon. Mother and Father fetched twigs and wood from the nearby dune bushes and started a fire, then set the billy to boil for tea. We ate the delicious warm scones Mother had baked earlier and wrapped in a white linen cloth, spread thick with melting butter and homemade strawberry jam.

Grandpa shook his head at the offer of a scone. Mother passed him a cup of sweet tea. His face was drawn and pale in the bright sunshine and he spoke little. Mother said he'd been that way ever since Grandma had died, leaving him alone at the store, the year before I was born. He grasped the enamel mug in both hands and smiled at her, a weary, wan smile, in contrast to the wheeling seagulls, the warm sand, and the sea that sparkled like diamonds.

'Doesn't that burn your hands, Grandpa?' I asked.

He smiled at me, a patient kindly smile. 'It warms my hands, sweetheart. And my heart too, I think.'

5

He wiped a smear of melted butter from my chin with a warm dry hand. The fingers were long, bony, the skin white like ivory. He sat, his hat askew on his head, the newly acquired stoop to his shoulders now evident, the flowing, grey-stippled beard framing his lean face. Father snapped the photograph that immortalised his illness.

I clearly remember my parents' conversation the day Grandpa was laid to rest. We were sitting around the kitchen table, an oil lamp throwing eerie forms on the white walls surrounding us. Grandpa's photograph, taken at Nahoon, lay on the table between us. I looked at it and thought of him, cold now in his grave. No cup of tea to warm his hands or his heart.

'I never realised he was so sick.' Mother's face twisted in anguish.

They had been to the lawyer's office to hear Grandpa's will read. It was a simple one. Grandpa had left his store to Mother.

'It's a windfall, Martha. We're rich.' Father's eyes had taken on a strange gleam. He patted her hand. 'Your father did well out of the store.'

Mother nodded. Her voice sounded broken, like she was choking over her words.

'But it wore him out. They worked so hard.' She blew her nose on a lace-edged white hanky. 'Mama died young; Papa wasn't old.'

Tears tracked twin paths down her cheeks. She hesitated, looking from Father to the photograph, then back again.

Eventually she sighed. 'All right then, Albert. We'll give it a go,' but her voice trembled with tears – or was it fear?

And so it was we left the safe confines of our little house in East London and journeyed first by train then by ox cart to Grandpa's store in the Transkei.

I remember the swaying train, the clickety-clack of the wheels on the track, pulling into a frosty station at night with lights blinking from uncurtained windows. Entering the hotel with its smells of tobacco, porridge, beer and old farts, then sticking my feet into cold, unfamiliar sheets, Fred wriggling beside me. Mother's lavender-scent as she tucked us in with a warm hand on our cheeks, each in turn.

She stood at the end of the bed, watching us, tall, serene, her lovely dark hair swept up to reveal an elegant neck encased in a high-necked blouse, the cameo brooch clasped at its centre. Her long skirt rustled as she tiptoed from the room to join Father in the bedroom next door.

We snuggled together. Fred breathed quietly beside me, the blankets pulled up under our chins, warmth seeping into our cold toes and up our legs.

The next morning we re-embarked on a train going east, rumbling across the mighty Kei River on a high rattly bridge. The Kei snaked through a deep valley, bounded on either side by craggy hills that rose up almost sheer and nude of plants apart from the bright aloes that flowered in season. Red, orange, like flames against the rock-strewn red soil laid bare by the goats.

Once clear of the valley we wound our way across huge plains where seas of grass undulated in waves of silver and green. The plains and valleys were studded with conical mud huts, topped by thatched roofs. Vast herds of cattle and scampering goats wandered at will. By that afternoon, we pulled into Dordrecht station and disembarked amidst a flurry of soot and the angry hiss of steam.

I remember my first sight of Ntando, the native man who was to become Father's right-hand man. How huge and strong he seemed, his grin ever-present. How his skin glowed shiny brown in the afternoon light as he helped Mother with our bags and eased her onto the cart while Father stood admiring a horse across the dusty street. Then we ground towards the store by ox cart, the red rumps plodding steadily.

As we journeyed further from Dordrecht, we gazed upon a ridge of mountains to the west. Their sheer rock faces were carved into intricate forms above a belt of dark trees resembling the fringe of hair beneath a monk's bald pate, before descending to steep grassed slopes. A river valley, curling languidly towards the ocean, striated the endless sea of grassy plains. Half-moons of grey dirt road crested each hill, linking the store to the civilised world.

I remember my first sight of the store. It was low-slung, a grey, squat, ugly building built of wattle and daub. A verandah, held up by crude wooden posts, spanned the breadth. To one side was a tank to collect rain water from the tin roof that would make us broil in summer and shiver in winter.

A rough railing made from hewn poles stood outside the store where visitors, destined to be so few and far between, could tether their mounts before entering.

A long line of natives stared at us with impassive eyes as we climbed down from the ox cart. The yard smelt of dust and manure.

Mother took our grimy palms in hers and led us past the immobile line. We waited while Father unlocked the door, eyeing the row of natives of all sizes. Father pushed it open and stood aside for us to enter. The interior smelt stale, musty. As if the air had followed us here from Grandpa's grave rather than being closed in with him.

There was a counter with shelves behind it. A door led off down a dank passage to the living quarters: a lounge, three bedrooms, a dining room and a kitchen.

The lounge was furnished in dark Victorian furniture, massive, impressive, oppressive. Heavy red curtains blocked out the light. Mother opened them and dust motes danced in the shaft of sunshine flooding into the room. She examined the photographs of Grandpa, Grandma and herself on the ornate mantelpiece, wiping grime from each loved face, touching their cold glass cheeks one by one.

Fred and I bounced on the overstuffed chairs.

'You'll ruin the furniture,' said Father with a stern look and we slid off, chastened.

11

We followed them down the passage to the bedrooms, each furnished with matching beds, huge walnut wardrobes and wrought iron filigree wash stands, still with their basins and jugs.

'Come,' Fred whispered to me, 'let's explore.'

And so we did, leaving via the back door to avoid the line of silent natives and climbing the slope of the hill behind the house and store. Puffing, we reached the top and turned to look back at our new home.

It stood alone in a barren landscape, unchanged by time's passing, crouched beneath a tall gum whispering secrets in a private wind. As I found out later, its yard, open to the world, changed with the seasons from dust to mud, churned up by wheels, hooves and feet, but was never fertile, destined never to foster life. It would suck the will from us all, numbing our growth.

Baptism of Fire

1914

Father and Fred left before the soft pinks of dawn streaked the sky. I could hear them stumbling in the dark before Mother lit the lamp, the muffled tread of their boots on the wooden floor, the faint bang as the door closed behind them, the scuffing hooves on the dirt yard, followed by hard riding towards the enlisting post, as though to flee the demons inhabiting the store. I heard Mother's stifled sobs and her blowing her nose on a handkerchief, before she washed at the stand on the other side of the wall.

13

Then all went silent as she made her way out of the house to the crude outhouse under the susurrating gum.

I waited until the first faint light of dawn brightened the curtain above my bed. I dressed quickly in the dark-blue cut-down dress I'd inherited from Mother, then splashed cold water onto hands and face at the washstand.

When I went through to the kitchen, Mother was in her usual place, floured to the elbows, her back stiff. I picked up the wood bucket and went out without speaking. A crow cawed from a low branch, and a reedbuck skittered, white-tailed, up the gentle slope behind the stables.

When I returned to the kitchen, Mother still stood with her back ramrod straight. Nontle came in behind me and greeted us both, then took the broom and went through the store to the verandah outside.

Mother slapped a bowl of porridge in front of me. I ate quickly and left to open the store. The younger boys came through later, jabbering, poking at each other as they left for the mission school.

At noon, when we'd closed the store for lunch, Ntando appeared at the kitchen door, his large hands clasping his hat's brim, bare brown feet etched with grey where soil had leaked into the crevices.

He greeted me deferentially. 'The cows and horses have no water.'

Over his shoulder, in the field beyond the outhouse and stables, I could see the huge milling bodies churning up dust near the trough. Water was Fred's department, a constant problem. The tank was too small, the trench from the spring on the mountain unreliable, the pipes he had been laying to circumvent the trench still not functional.

I turned to Mother. She looked away. Nontle was at the stove, stirring mealie meal porridge in a big black pot.

'What do you need to repair the water?'

'A wrench, from Master Fred's toolbox.' He pointed to the wooden box sitting in the corner of the kitchen near Father's comfy chair.

'Come in, find what you need.' I held the door open for him.

He glanced quickly at Mother, then at Nontle as he entered unfamiliar territory. He bent over the toolbox, squatting on his haunches as he turned over each tool with a metallic clatter until he found the one he wanted.

He held it up to me with a gap-toothed grin, brown tobacco-stained stubs inside a pink mouth.

'I'll come out with you,' I said.

He led the way, shoulders hunched in his ill-fitting coat – a cast-off of Father's – tan corduroy breeches riding up thin brown ankles, bare calloused feet encrusted with grey. We went past the stables, through the crude concertina gate fashioned from barbed wire and rough bent poles that had been hacked from the bush lining the ravines that criss-crossed the plains. Ntando leant over the trough and worked steadily. With a hiss and a rush, brown water shot from the valve and splashed against the end of the trough, drenching Ntando in an instant. Ignoring it, he turned to me with a grin and began to

16

assemble the valve, bringing the gush to a manageable flow that tempted the horses and cattle to move forward, where they slurped noisily at the cool water filling the trough.

'Ntando! Come quickly!' Nontle's voice was a quavery shriek that sent chills down my spine.

She was running down the path towards the field, eyes wide, gesturing towards the hills to our left. A group of piccaninnies ran after her, laughing, pointing. A billow of black smoke rose above the green grass, boiling, angry – coming from the direction of the mission school. *The boys! The Gordons!* We'd have to inspan the horses and load the cart with buckets of water to fight the fire.

Ntando was through the gate before me, gathering harness and traces from inside the stable, racing back towards the horses.

Mother was shouting. 'Help me, Eve. Wet these sacks.' She held hessian sacks in both hands.

I ran up the path and joined Mother at the water tank, where we pushed the sacks under the precious flow, turning the dust in the sacks to a paste that clung to our hands and feet.

'We'll have to run. Ntando and the piccaninnies can bring the cart round on the road later, when they've filled the buckets.'

We left Nontle at the house, wringing her hands.

Our breath rasped in our throats as we laboured up the hill towards the mission station. I soon outstripped Mother, and turned back to wait as she struggled up the steep hill in her long, cumbersome skirt. She gestured for me to go ahead, her breath coming in huge gasps, hair tumbling from its strict confines around her pale cheeks.

I ran fleet as a reedbuck with a leopard at its tail. As I crested the last hill, I looked down on the mission station. The buildings were made of wattle and daub, like the store, but unlike the store and our home, they had thatched roofs made from the tall grass that flourished on the hillsides.

Smoke billowed from the Gordon's house. The thatch was well alight, flames with sharp red, orange and yellow tongues flickering through the thatch, framed against the brilliant cobalt of an African sky. Reverend Gordon and some of the natives who lived at the mission were in the home paddock filling buckets from a trough, passing the water-filled containers along a human chain and throwing them on the fire, trying to quell the flames. Their efforts were futile. More and more of the roof was consumed in a cloud of grey and black smoke that ballooned into the sky far above their heads.

Julia Gordon stood outside the school with her brood of scholars, the array of brown arms and legs broken only by the stark white limbs of our four boys. They babbled excitedly, watching the flames leap into the sky. The smoke swelled in bursts like the sails of a wind-driven galleon.

A burning ember flicked across in the wind generated by the fire-storm, landing innocuously on the broad swath of thatch that formed the roof of the school room. The ember lay dormant for a second, then flared, took root, and bloomed into a red flower of flame that crackled and smoked as it began to consume the dry grass.

19

'The roof!' I shouted, pointing.

I raced down the hill, the long grass on the edge of the path whipping my bare legs where I held my skirt high. I arrived, breathless, to stand next to Julia, who was gazing up at the burgeoning flames with near despair.

'Do you have more water?' I gasped.

She shook her head. 'There's nothing we can do. Not against this. It's too dangerous, my dear.' Her voice cracked in a sob.

The damp sack hung limp in my hand.

The children gesticulated wildly, high piping shrieks coming from immature vocal chords.

'Come away!' I shouted, pulling at their coats.

The children craned their necks to see the flames devouring the roof of their school house. The thatch on the Gordon's house spat and flared, the roar like a steam train, fearsome.

'Where's Cliffie?' Mother gasped as she arrived at my side.

I looked around. Bert, Tom and Eddie were with the piccaninnies, chattering excitedly as they watched the thatch disappear into long flakes of soot that spun into the air like black snow.

'He was here a minute ago.' I glanced quickly at the bobbing heads, then lifted my gaze towards the school house.

We all saw it at the same instant. A flitting shadow silhouetted against the bright glow of the flames – inside the school!

'Cliff!' I yelled, as we all ran forward.

The thatch on the Gordon's house collapsed with a crash into the flames consuming their house. The fire roared louder, the cracks like the clapping of a cheering crowd.

The heat drove us back, burning our faces, making our hair fan and wither.

'Cliffie!' Mother wailed.

Then a dark form in an ill-fitting coat surged past us. Ntando held his arm up to his forehead to protect his eyes and ran, head-down, towards the figure inside the school. He leapt through the burning doorframe into the fiery inferno, his silhouette distorting in the heat-haze from the fire.

21

He stumbled, but then he regained his feet and surged towards where Cliff's tiny shape now huddled against the cupboard that had housed Julia's teaching aids.

Ntando leant forward, reaching strong arms for Cliff, but was pushed back by burning thatch falling in a fireball between them. Ntando turned back, bent double as he coughed in the choking smoke, then he straightened, seemed to gather strength, and surged past the burning heap to where Cliff now lay prostrate on the ground.

He scooped up Cliff's limp body and ran back, dodging the glowing embers that rained down around them. The doorframe was blazing fiercely now, completely engulfed in flames. There was no way through.

Ntando hesitated, holding Cliff's young body like an offering before the altar of some crazed god. He raised his eyes heavenwards and we feared he would collapse there, yielding to the inferno. But then he forged through, head down, shielding Cliff's body with his own, blindly leaping through the flames surrounding the doorframe.

He arrived, panting, wild gaze showing the whites of his eyes, and collapsed on the bare ground away from the heat, his wet coat steaming.

'Cliffie!' Ntando released Cliff into Mother's waiting arms.

Cliff coughed as he woke up. His face was blackened, eyes grey-green pools against sooty cheeks. His spiky blond hair was singed at the edges. Otherwise, he seemed unharmed.

Julia turned to Ntando. He sat on the bare earth, his face contorted in agony. His hat had fallen into the fire, his peppercorn curls crinkled into auburn bobbles by the heat. His yellow-brown complexion was streaked with soot. But it was his feet that had taken the brunt. Burnt flesh hung in tatters where his soles had touched the embers.

'I'll fetch bandages.' Julia turned away as if to run to her house, as was her custom in the face of injury. Then she stopped, looked at the ruined walls, flames still leaping from the poles and thatch that had fallen in upon the contents. Bare bones of furniture stood, skeletal, charred, twisting in the heat haze as flames licked at them, entreating them to join the dancing soot and smoke rising into the air.

She turned back to us and shrugged, a gesture of helplessness, hopelessness. Years of work smouldered behind her.

Ntando held the tops of his feet in his hands, rocking back and forth, his knees bent out sideways, Buddha-like, face twisted in pain.

'What were you doing, Cliffie?' Mother held him close.

'Mrs Gordon's teaching aids are in there. What will she do without them?' He began to wail.

'Oh, Cliffie! Things don't matter, they can be replaced. It's people that matter. Isn't that what we've taught you?' Mother touched his cheek with a soot-blackened hand, tracing the pink runnels where tears had washed his cheeks clean.

'But if the school's gone, the Gordons won't stay! How will we learn anything? We'll never get away from here!'

Julia regarded him silently and then straightened her shoulders as she turned to watch Ken directing the natives where to throw water onto the roof of the chapel.

But it was futile. The flames flickered onto the thatch and steamed at them as they threw water, but the fire only hesitated, then gathered ferocity and licked and flickered and ate at will, consuming the thatch in an angry conflagration. They finally stopped, knowing they'd lost, and just watched.

We all stood helpless as the flames finished their work, laying bare the house, the school, the chapel. Even the piccaninnies were hushed, and the only sound was the crackle and roar of the flames consuming what was left of the buildings. Overhead circled vultures and storks, wheeling in the thermals created by the smoke.

When only the blackened, stark skeletons of the buildings remained, and thin wisps of smoke curled into the air, we loaded all that was ours.

We had to lift Ntando onto the cart. He clenched his teeth, but uttered no sound. Only the beads of sweat on his yellow-brown brow bore testimony to his pain. Cliff sat up front with Mother, while the younger boys took the shortcut over the hills, accompanied by a crowd of piccaninnies discussing the fate of the mission.

I stood with the Gordons, surveying the ruins of their life. Julia was stoical, but her stricken eyes belied her brave face.

'We'll wait for the cart to return, shall we?' I asked gently.

Reverend Gordon answered. 'No, no, there's no use in that. We can walk. There's nothing wrong with our legs, you know. It's the buildings that're damaged.'

Damaged? I looked at the charred remnants. Nothing was salvageable. They would have to start from scratch.

We made a sorry sight, trailing over the hills towards the store, me leading the way.

We entered our house via the store and I took the Gordons through to the kitchen, where Mother and Nontle were bent over Ntando's groaning form. He sat on a kitchen chair while they smeared creamy white honey onto his badly burnt feet.

'This will stop infection,' Mother was saying. 'It must be white honey, though. Once it's boiled, it's no good for wounds.'

Talking stopped her thinking. I knew how she felt. With the men gone and now Ntando out of commission, how would we manage? Reverend Gordon? He wasn't much of a handyman – he was too scholarly. Fred had been doing repairs for him at the mission for years.

Julia bent over Ntando's feet. I think she needed to feel useful. They had taken Ntando's jacket off and it lay across the back of the chair, his thin chest hunched over in the threadbare white shirt. His corduroy breeches were pushed up to the knees while Mother and Julia bandaged his feet with thick white strips torn from old bed sheets.

He winced as they tugged at them, but the white women didn't seem to notice. Only Nontle watched his eyes, closed against the pain at times, and patted his large bony hand with her small fluttering one.

Her eyes flicked between his face and his feet, watching as the white snake coiled itself around his yellow-brown legs.

The Line in the Sand

In the end, the line in the sand for us came suddenly.

After the horror of Ron and Ross' experience in the township a few weeks' before, we had decided on a new path in life.

With this in mind, we went down to the south coast of Natal to a place called Annerley, where we'd seen a macadamia farm advertised. I can't remember which came first: a trip to Australia which gave us the idea of farming macadamias; or a trip to Australia because of our interest in farming macadamias.

The upshot, though, was that we phoned the agent and made an appointment to see the house and farm. It was a glorious Midlands day when we set off, the dew sparkling on the remaining rye grass, the sun warm but not hot, the sky a cerulean blue dotted with fluffy white clouds. Giant's Castle, part of the southern Drakensberg, which dominated our view on the western horizon, serrated the heavens like a sharp fang.

After a two-hour drive, we arrived at the sleepy seaside village of Annerley and wound up through the narrow, leafy, rain-sodden roads to the top of the coastal escarpment where the agent was to meet us.

Our first impression of the house was favourable. It was spacious and light with a view out towards the cobalt canvas of sea framed by the tall milkwood trees that grew in this area.

Below us stretched the deep rich green of the macadamias. I don't remember much about the property other than the impression of peace, light and tranquillity. There was a feeling of luxuriant abundance that was instantly appealing, and I could see myself living there.

Ever cautious, we didn't make a hasty decision. We asked our sons and their prospective wives to give us their opinion and so it was the following Saturday that we all headed down the coast to inspect the property once more.

Their exclamations of approval only confirmed our initial impression: this was a beautiful house and a very viable property.

In keeping with our cautious approach to making major decisions, we went home and discussed the pros and cons in detail over a late lunch of cold meat, salad and crusty bread. By mid-afternoon, the decision was made: we would phone the agent come Monday and tell him we'd decided to buy. Feeling lighter than I'd done in years, I gathered our troop of hounds and set off, this time on foot, to check on our heavily pregnant heifers which at that time were grazing in one of our old ryegrass paddocks close to the main road.

By this time more clouds scudded across the azure sky and a brisk breeze bowed the tall grass and rustled the leaves of the sweet-scented wattle trees as I passed under them.

I found the group of heifers fairly easily and began to count, checking as I did so that all looked fit and healthy. The dogs had fanned out in small groups, sniffing along the trails of buck, hares and rodents.

Eighteen heifers.

I frowned. There should be twenty.

I counted again.

Eighteen.

Puzzled, I headed towards the gum trees growing in the middle of the field, thinking the missing two might be lying in the shade, though on such a relatively cool day it was unlikely. I also had a sinking feeling growing in the pit of my stomach. We'd had so many cattle thefts over the years. Was this another incident?

Besides the considerable monetary value of these heifers (at that time probably about R5000 each, which was top dollar, as they were well bred and carrying calves from the best international sires available), I could never bear the cruelty that was meted out to stolen cattle and was likely to be meted out to them if they had indeed been stolen. The thought of them being slaughtered in the most inhumane way possible made me shudder.

I reached the trees and looked around. Nothing. The comforting sound of the wind in the trees now sounded like malicious whispering.

With growing dread I scouted the surrounding area. Then I noticed four of the dogs gathered at a spot closer to the main road. Heart thumping, dread and anger growing, I ran towards them, mentally cursing my lack of agility in the long tangling grass and wishing fervently that I'd had the good sense to ride a horse.

As I drew nearer I could see flies rising in swarms from something concealed in the grass. A strong smell drifted to me, at once metallic, but also putrid, almost faecal. Fearing what I would find, I moved closer. Blood, copious blood. Two patches. And only metres further on, the intestines and stomach contents of two beasts.

There was little doubt as to the fate of the heifers.

Continued ...

A Bittersweet Decision

As I stood there, gazing at what remained of our precious animals, sadness, then shock and revulsion flooded through me. It was as though someone had slogged me in the stomach with a ten-foot pole. I doubled over and dry-retched into the grass. When I recovered, I called the dogs to me and stumbled away from the scene on legs that felt too weak to carry me.

The trip back to the house seemed to take a long time, much longer than it had on the way out. As we passed the group of grazing heifers, I did a quick mental check to see if I could pinpoint which of them had met such a horrible end. The cattle had always been individuals to me. Having cared for them literally since the day they were born, I knew each one intimately – her parents and grandparents, her date of birth, milestones in her development, in fact her entire life history. I loved them in a way that went beyond practicality.

Weighed down by my feelings, I arrived back at the house at last, the dogs still in tow, and told Ron and our boys what I had found. Dave, a senior police officer with the stock theft unit, lived on a neighbouring farm, so we phoned him and told him what had happened. He agreed to meet us at our road end.

Grim-faced, we all set out once more, this time crowded into and onto a pickup truck, to see if we could figure out exactly what had happened.

Dave was waiting for us.

We parked near the main road, greeted him and then set off together on foot to investigate.

Ron spotted something immediately. 'There. See. A truck has reversed up here.' He pointed to where the long thatch grass had been laid over in twin tracks. 'I'm surprised we didn't see it this morning when we went out.'

But we hadn't been looking for anything suspicious that morning; we'd been happy: laughing, talking, distracted, looking forward to the trip down the coast.

We followed the path the truck had taken. It had reversed right up against the fence, using the low bank below the fence to form a natural loading ramp.

'See. They've cut the wires here.' Ron pointed again to where strands of barbed wire were missing from the fence.

I cursed under my breath. We were lucky the remaining eighteen hadn't wandered onto the main road and been struck by a vehicle. During another stock theft incident on a neighbouring farm some years before, the fence onto the main road had also been cut and a huge truck had ploughed into the neighbour's herd, killing half a dozen cattle, fortunately no people.

We walked on until we reached the spot where the heifers had been slaughtered. Dave strolled from one site to the other, his hand on his chin. I wrinkled my nose against the noisome smell and swallowed the bile threatening to choke me.

'I've seen this before, an incident last week up near Nottingham Road,' Dave said at last. 'They're a new gang, we think.'

He indicated the patches of blood.

'They appear to shoot the cattle, and then cut their throats. That's why there's so much blood. Then they cut them open and take out the stomach contents.' He gestured towards the two fly-covered piles that lay reeking in the late-afternoon sun. 'Then they use the wire they've cut from the fence to tow the bodies to where their truck is waiting and pull the bodies aboard. We think they gut them to make the carcasses lighter.' He straightened and sighed, and then wiped his hand over his face.

With this information in mind, we looked about once more. Now that he'd mentioned it and we knew to look, we could quite clearly see the drag marks where the heifers' bodies had been towed towards the fence. The grass was still slightly flattened.

We thanked Dave and accompanied him back to his vehicle.

As we walked, I considered this new state of affairs. We'd never had a case like this before, and it marked a new low in our lives, with the already prevalent incidences of stock and other types of theft probably set to escalate.

Was this what we had to look forward to? And if so, could we survive financially?

Dave stood beside his vehicle, door open, one foot resting on the foot-well, and promised to follow up on the case, but as we watched him drive away we didn't hold out much hope. Despite the good work they tried to do, they seldom caught anyone.

Feeling glum, we repaired the fence with wire and tools that were always in the truck, and then returned home, our excited chatter from earlier in the day now converted to gloomy silence.

I prepared a quick supper of boiled eggs and toast. As we sat down to eat we began to discuss the events of the day.

Eventually, after much back and forth, we came to a decision.

We looked at each other in silence and then Ron voiced our thoughts.

'We can't continue to farm here in Merrivale. The security situation is escalating out of control and the stealing is crippling us. And both are only going to get worse. We've considered moving down to the coast to farm macadamias. From research we've done, we know that farming macadamias in South Africa has one major problem: theft.'

He took a deep breath and exhaled in a rush.

'After what's happened today, there doesn't seem much point in buying a macadamia farm in South Africa. We'd only swap one set of thieves for another. If we're going to make such a radical change, it's best we go and farm macadamias in Australia.'

And so the bittersweet decision was made.

The Red Shirt and the Dolphin

I stood with my legs leaning against the rough concrete wall, my face to the rising sun. Before me, on waves turned translucent in the early morning light, surfers rode the swell. Hand to my brow, I scanned the breakers.

He wasn't there.

Shoulders slumped, I turned to resume my walk.

'Were you looking for someone?' She had twinkly cobalt eyes set in a lined pixie face.

'Yep. I was, in fact. A young guy, 'bout my age, here every day. He wears a red T-shirt and he surfs with a dolphin.'

She smiled. 'That'll be Matt.'

'You know him?'

'Kind of. I know the man who sponsors him.'

I raised my eyebrows.

'Larry Thornton. He used to be here every day too.'

She must have noticed my puzzled expression.

'An old man? Ninety-three, sits in a wheelchair near the surf lifesaving club, watching the waves?'

Light dawned. 'Oh, yes. I've seen him. He hasn't been there for a few days either.' A frown crumpled my brow. 'Is he okay?'

'Oh, he's okay. He just can't get here, is all. His carer, or rather the lady who always brought him here, met with ... misfortune.'

'Sorry to hear that,' I murmured, glancing back out to sea. 'Is Matt a famous surfer then? Is he someone I should know?'

'You're not from around here?'

'I'm from down south, but I live here now. I'm studying Social Science at uni.'

'A girl who wants to help people then?'

I nodded and my cheeks felt hot.

'Do you know how this came to be?' She touched the rough concrete wall in front of us.

'Was it a tidal pool?'

She shook her head. 'It was a dolphin pool.'

I looked at the shallow water. 'It must have been a lot deeper then.'

'It was. The coastline has changed considerably since it was built. The first dolphins were caught in the wild, put into these pools and taught to perform. People used to flock here to watch them. This place was famous.'

She paused and sipped from her water bottle. I could see the pride in her face as she looked at the remains of the dolphin pool walls. A wave rushed in and spread over the rocks in a creamy white foam.

I licked my lips; they tasted of salt from the sea. 'I'm sorry, but how does this affect Matt? We were talking about him ...'

44

She peered at me. 'It's a long story. Do you have time?'

I glanced at my phone. 'I don't have to be at uni till nine.'

She gave a strange smile. 'Matt's a special person; an admirable man.'

I waited.

'Perhaps I should start with Larry Thornton.'

I shrugged. I was impatient to learn more about Matt, but it was her story, not mine.

'In his young days, Larry was an avid surfer, in the water every day at first light. He was only nineteen when war broke out in 1939 but by that time he had a young wife and a three-month-old son. Leaving them must have been hard, but he enlisted and was sent to North Africa.' She pursed her lips. 'Unfortunately, Larry was captured early on in the campaign there and spent the rest of the war in a prisoner-of-war camp in Germany. I believe he suffered terribly.'

I remained silent, watching the surfers as they cut through the water. A seagull screeched overhead.

'When he left, he was your typical Aussie bloke: young, carefree, loved a good time. The man who came back to Australia was emaciated, mean and morose. His son Billy was six years old by that time and had no memory of his father. The gaunt stranger who returned to live with them was like a monster to him. He looked scary and he acted worse.

'Despite his condition, though, Larry hit the ground running. He had a wife and son to provide for and he was determined to do that well. Before the war, he'd worked in a timber yard: hard, physical work. After the war, he became an entrepreneur.'

I raised my eyebrows. 'How? What did he do?'

'He began making clothing and handbags – high-end stuff – and they sold like hotcakes, here and overseas.' She beamed with pride.

I smiled. I couldn't picture the old man I'd seen in the wheelchair as someone who would make clothing and handbags, but what matter? Good on him. It was different – and inspiring.

'He proved to be an astute businessman, ruthless, smart, and he became really wealthy.' She frowned.

'The only problem was he treated his poor wife May and Billy very badly: always angry, always finding fault, always shouting at them.' She sighed. 'The power and money went to his head. He didn't appreciate what he had, thought he could treat his wife and son like he did his employees: with disdain. No one liked him and I think most people were afraid of him, but money gave him power, you know, and that makes people kowtow.'

An outrigger canoe rounded the headland, the rowers' oars dipping and rising in unison.

My companion continued. 'Larry had no time for his family or friends, or to go back to the waves. His business and succeeding became more important.'

'How do you know all this?' I said.

She smiled. 'My mother Lillian was May's best friend. May used to tell my mother everything.' She turned to stare out at the breakers. 'Billy remained an only child – a lonely child. Larry was determined his son would take over the business one day, but he didn't want the boy to have a "free ride", as he put it. Billy would have to work for his wealth, just as

47

Larry had done. So friends for Billy were out of the question.'

'How awful,' I murmured, trailing my fingers across the rough sea wall.

'Yes, it was.' She tossed her head and flicked a stray strand of hair from her forehead. 'By the time Billy was nineteen, he had been working for his father for a year and was being groomed to take a leading role. But the young man's heart wasn't in it. Not then. He was spending most of his free time in the surf – just like his father had done.

She took another sip of her water. A wave hit the rocks with a sound like a thunderclap. Spray and salt tang filled the air.

'In 1959, not long after the dolphin pool was built, Larry had an appointment with an important overseas buyer. The only problem was, it meant a trip to the city and the tycoon wanted to meet Larry's family as well: Billy because he was being groomed to take over the business, and May because the tycoon had brought his wife with him too.

'On the morning they were to travel up to the city, Billy was down here, surfing. Larry came down to fetch him, furious because Billy should have known better than to sneak off for a surf when they had a meeting to go to.

'When Larry arrived at the beach, he had no trouble spotting Billy. He always wore a red shirt to protect his skin – he was fair like his mother. Larry shouted to Billy but it took a while before he could attract the boy's attention and he grew angrier with each passing minute. As he watched, he noticed a wild dolphin swimming beside his son. Whenever Billy stood to surf, the dolphin would appear on the crest of the wave and surf in with him. They did this time and again, until Larry managed to catch his attention. Then Billy came out of the waves – right away.

'But it wasn't quick enough for Larry. By the time Billy was at his side, Larry was furious. The boy still had to shower and change, and they would be late for the appointment. He yelled at Billy and wouldn't listen as Billy tried to tell him his theory about the dolphin – that the owner of the dolphin pool had caught its mate and it was lonely, needing a friend. Larry just kept checking his watch, telling the boy to hurry. Then he struck him – full across the face. The blow left a red mark on the boy's cheek, and May, who had left the car by this stage and was standing beside them, covered her face with her hands and began to cry.'

My companion paused to wipe the corner of her eye with a tissue, before slipping it back into the pocket of her shorts.

In a gruffer voice, she continued. 'The trip to the city was a nightmare. Larry was trying to make up time and he drove too fast. In a dip halfway there, he lost control of the car. It flipped over and over. The sound of tearing metal and breaking glass seemed to go on forever. Eventually it came to rest upside down, the only sound the hiss of water leaking from the engine and the sound of the wheels spinning in the air.' Her voice was subdued now.

'Larry was alone in the car. May and Billy had been thrown out. He was in immense pain, his leg at a grotesque angle, and the pain was so bad he almost passed out. With a gargantuan effort, he forced the buckled driver's door open and rolled out onto the grass. He could smell the hot engine oil and taste blood in his mouth. Dragging his leg, he crawled back towards the road. He found May first. She was in the long grass not far from the edge of the road. The car had rolled over her. She was still alive, but only just. He did what he could for her and then crawled on to find Billy. By the time he spied the boy lying on the road, another vehicle had stopped and a man was out of his car, bending over him.

'Larry dragged himself to them. As soon as he drew closer, he could see Billy was dead. By the time an ambulance arrived, May was dead too. In such a short time, Larry had gone from a man who had everything to a man who had nothing, nothing that really counted for much. And all he could think of was how he had ignored what Billy was trying to tell him and that stinging slap to the boy's cheek.'

She sighed. 'He never did make his appointment and eventually lost his leg, amputated below the knee.'

I inhaled sharply.

'You never noticed, heh?' She smiled at me.

I shook my head.

'I suppose you wouldn't. When he's sitting in his wheelchair near the surf club, he always has a blanket over his knees.'

I nodded. 'I just thought he was old, felt the cold more than the rest of us.' I thought about what had happened to Larry. 'How would anyone recover from what he'd done?'

She shrugged. 'He had to. It took him a while, but he learnt to walk again. As soon as he could, he sold the business for a fat profit and returned to the sea, learning to surf again on only one leg.'

'A pity it took the loss of his wife and son to show him he needed to do things differently.'

She nodded, and then her eyes twinkled. 'You'll never guess what he did too ...'

I shook my head.

'He wore a red shirt in Billy's honour and in no time Billy's dolphin joined him. From then on, every day, if he wore the red shirt, a dolphin would join him. Years later, in a speech he gave to up-and-coming entrepreneurs, he said that his experience with the dolphins after causing the death of his wife and son had taught him many things, but the most important were to cherish the "now" and value what is important.'

I peered out at the waves, hoping that I would see the distinctive grey-brown of a dolphin's hump, but there was nothing, just the unceasing motion of the ocean as it breathed and sighed.

'Not long after that he started a foundation to help boys from troubled backgrounds. He made it his life's work to mentor them by teaching them to surf and, through contact with the dolphins, to embrace the healing power of their love and acceptance. He was an inspiration to them, because if he could learn to forgive himself for what had happened to May and Billy, and he could learn to surf on one leg, they learnt that almost anything is possible. He funded their education, helped them secure good jobs. Through the years, many have gone on to be solid citizens, and they in turn mentor boys, but of course not using the dolphins. That's Larry's thing; his and his latest mentee's.'

'So that's the sponsorship you mentioned?'

She nodded.

'How does it work? I mean, Larry's too old to teach anyone to surf now. How does Matt fit in?'

'When Larry was too old to teach the boys to surf anymore, one or two of his mentees took over from him here. They take it in turns to teach boys who need help.'

'But Matt looks young to be a mentor. Is that what he does?'

Her neatly plucked brows knitted. 'Maybe one day; he's still healing; he's not quite there yet. He's Larry's latest protégé, and one of his previous protégés is teaching him to surf.'

I hesitated and then asked the question that was on my mind. 'What's his problem?'

She took a while to reply. 'He comes from an abusive background. His father was wealthy, influential, but he treated Matt and his mother appallingly.' She gave an ironic smile. 'Sounds like a repeat of Larry's story, doesn't it?'

I nodded and pressed closer to the sea wall to allow some early-morning walkers to pass.

'I'm sorry,' I said, 'but I still don't completely understand why Larry no longer comes to watch. And where is Matt?'

Her eyes glistened. 'Have you read the papers in the last few days, listened to the news?'

I thought a while then realisation dawned. 'You mean ...?'

The corners of her lips turned down. 'Yes. The woman who was shot was Matt's mother. The assailant was her rich and famous husband, Matt's father. Did you read the full story?'

I shook my head. 'No. I saw it on the news, but I hardly listened.'

She pursed her lips. 'When Matt was only sixteen, Matt's father was hitting his mother and Matt intervened. He got between them and undoubtedly saved his mother's life, but in the process sustained such a severe beating himself that it left him brain-damaged.'

My jaw dropped open and I watched as a wave hissed in over the rocks and then retreated back down a channel.

She grunted. 'Oh, he's a fighter. Like I told you: he's a brave young man and admirable. He's working hard on his rehabilitation. At first he couldn't walk properly and he battled with his balance and the hearing in one ear, but he's coming along nicely. It's taken him three long years but he's almost there. I think he went to his first job interview only the other day.' She smiled and then lines formed on her brow. 'His father went to jail for what he had done, but was released only last week. It took him no time at all to track Matt and his mother down. He found out where they lived and shot her. Matt was out with friends at the time so he was lucky to survive, but he found her when he came home. A gruesome sight, I believe.'

A coldness crept over me, despite the mildness of the morning. 'So where is Matt, then?'

'Probably at home, dealing with things. What happened to his mother would be hard to process.'

'And Larry?'

She shrugged. 'At the old-age home. Without Matt's mother Linda to help him, there's no one to bring him here.'

I stared at her, assimilating her words.

We spoke for a few minutes more, and then she sucked on her water bottle again and checked her watch.

'It's quarter past eight,' she said, and you still have to get to uni.' She smiled.

'I'd better get going,' I said. 'Thanks for telling me the story.'

We parted and I set off for the long walk to my unit. Before I rounded the corner at the headland, though, I turned back to gaze towards the bay again, hoping to catch sight of perhaps a red shirt or the grey-brown back of a dolphin. But there was nothing, just the hard outline of what had been the porpoise pool silhouetted against the stark blue of the morning sky.

A few days later we met again, this time in front of the surf club.

'Hello, dear. I thought it might be you.' She leant forward and shouted, 'Beautiful morning, Larry. Glad to see you out again.'

Larry looked up at her with blank and rheumy eyes.

'It's Judy, Larry. You remember? My mother Lillian was friends with your late wife May?' She winked at me.

Larry's blank look cleared and he smiled, a quavery, watery smile that twisted the corners of his lips.

'Are you enjoying being out again?' Judy's voice boomed above the sound of the waves.

Larry nodded and resumed his stare out to sea.

Judy turned to me.

I smiled, my hands resting on the handles of Larry's wheelchair.

'So you found him?' She spoke softly this time.

'Yes, your directions were clear,' I said as I checked that the brake was engaged on the wheelchair.

'Did you get to see Matt's mother Linda?'

I straightened. 'She's still in hospital, but the wound is healing well. She should be out soon.'

She looked me straight in the eye. 'And you found Matt too.'

We both turned back to the ocean. I smiled as a glassy swell built out to sea. Then a figure wearing a distinctive red shirt stood to ride the wave to the shallows. Beside him, just ahead of the curl of the breaker, was the unmistakeable grey-brown shape of a dolphin, its upturned mouth for all the world looking as though it was smiling.

'Yes,' I grinned. 'I found Matt too.'

Green is the Colour

'You'll never guess who I bumped into today, Des.' Ruth's voice intruded into my thoughts.

I dragged my eyes away from the news and forced myself to focus on her words. 'No, who?' I tried to feign interest.

'Maggie.'

An instant image of Maggie with her lithe figure, short blonde hair and green cat's eyes flashed into my mind. But that Maggie was long gone, as I remembered her from at least thirty years ago.

'Maggie who?' I said, turning back to my tablet.

'Maggie Kendall, your ex-wife! Here in Toowoomba.' Ruth never failed to amaze me. There was no hint of triumph or disdain, no jealousy. She sounded genuinely pleased.

'Oh,' I said. 'That's a surprise.'

When I'd seen Maggie and Roger downtown the other day, I hadn't told Ruth. I'd hoped they were just passing through. Perhaps they were; perhaps they were just visiting someone from the old country. Lord knows, there were enough of us ex-patriots around.

'They've migrated here. They're looking to buy into a business.'

I tried to concentrate on what I was reading, but realised I was wasting my time. 'Here in Toowoomba?' I blinked at Ruth, hoping my shock looked like surprise.

'Yes. Poor things have had such a hard time it seems.' As Ruth babbled on, elaborating on what had happened to Maggie and Roger since we'd last seen them, I drifted away to the past.

If Roger had fallen on hard times, so be it. It wasn't as if he didn't deserve it. It was about time he came short.

I thought back to when Maggie and I had first met. We'd both been kids at school, she a year younger than I was and attending a boys' school because the girls' school didn't offer maths. She'd always been a bright spark, clever and funny and completely captivating. I knew from the first time I set eyes on her in her short school tunic that she was the girl for me. As luck would have it, she chose me too, and when we'd both finished our studies, we'd married.

Of course we were different by then, no longer the innocent kids who had met at school. In our tortured and war-torn country, we both experienced some terrible things. Maggie was a nurse and mid-wife, while I was a plumber and saw service in the army.

It was there I met Roger.

And more fool me I introduced him to Maggie, my beautiful, kind, compassionate Maggie. She was no match for his charms. He had doe eyes, soft and brown, and lashes that swept his cheeks when he looked down at his feet. He was an impressive specimen, tall, with broad shoulders and a haunted air about him that women, especially, found attractive. He spun this tale about how his family had been killed in a terrorist raid and he had been the only one to survive. It was all rubbish, of course, as I found out much later, but for someone as soft-hearted as Maggie, that was the clincher. She felt protective towards him and caught up in his tragedy.

Still, even though I knew they were close, I never suspected it of him – or of her. Most certainly not of her. She was the love of my life, the emerald-eyed mother of my future children.

So when I came home to find them together in our lounge, sitting conspiratorially close, their thighs touching, I wasn't even suspicious. I didn't like it, mind, but he was my best friend and she was my wife. I loved them both.

'Beer?' I asked Roger, holding out a cold one I'd fetched from the fridge.

'Yeah, sure. Thanks.' He cracked the cap off with ease.

Maggie stood and went through to the kitchen. When she came back she was clutching some wine. She stood in the doorway, leaning against the frame, one small foot balanced on the other.

'What's up?' I asked, judging from their poses they had something to tell me.

They looked at me in silence. I took a swig of my beer. The bitter taste washed away the heat and dust of the day.

Maggie came and sat down next to Roger. I can still remember the frown as it crumpled my brow. Why had she sat next to him and not me?

But the thought had barely formed when she said, 'Roger and I are in love. We want to be together.'

Whoa! In love. My head and heart reeled. Maggie loved me, not Roger. My mouth gaped like a fish out of water.

They stood.

'Where are you going?' I croaked.

Maggie gave a half-smile. Was it compassion or sorrow for what she was doing? 'I'm leaving you, Des. It's over between us.'

Then they walked out, leaving me with the aftermath, still unable to comprehend what had happened. Oh, I raged and I ranted, I fell into depression, I even, at one time, considered taking my life. The worst of it was, not only had Roger taken my wife and my life, but I also had to continue to go on patrols with him for the next umpteen years. And oh how I hated him. Many's the time I considered pulling the trigger on that smarmy deceitful back, but somehow I refrained.

And in time I met Ruth. She was nothing like Maggie. She had fiery red hair and eyes the colour of amber, and a tall statuesque figure that dwarfed Maggie's petite frame.

Once the war was over we went our separate ways. Ruth and I concentrated on building our business while Maggie and Roger did who knows what. Rumours flew that they were into prospecting then mining and then into import and export.

Whatever it was, they were doing well. Good on them. While Ruth and I struggled to make ends meet and raise our three children together, Maggie and Roger lived the high life, childless but rich beyond anything we could imagine.

Then one day, as I was returning to the business from a job in the suburbs, who should I see standing on the footpath but Maggie. She was wringing her hands and pacing up and down, glancing left and right as she walked.

I approached her warily. I hadn't seen her in years, but she still looked devastating and that familiar ache of loss I'd tried so hard to suppress was back with a vengeance.

'Oh, Des,' she said as soon as she saw me. 'I've been waiting for you for ages.' Her words were quick and nervous, her green eyes moist with unshed tears.

My resolve melted. 'What is it, Maggie? What's happened?' I longed to scoop her into my arms and hold her tight against my heart, to feel the softness of her and smell the scent of her hair.

'Can we talk inside?' She glanced about her once again.

Grudgingly, I nodded, and opened the door for her to precede me. Ruth would be inside, and my precious opportunity to be alone with Maggie would come to an end.

Ruth raised her eyebrows at me, but welcomed Maggie politely. It was obvious to her that my ex-wife was in distress. We closed and locked the door and then listened as Maggie explained.

'It's Roger. He's in trouble. Emeralds. He's been smuggling emeralds and we've had word the cops are going to arrest him. Early tomorrow morning when we're both asleep!' She covered her face with her hands and her shoulders shook as she sobbed. In time she looked up, her cheeks shiny with tears.

'Please can you help him, Des. Please! I'll die if anything happens to him. Can you help him get out of the country before they catch him?'

A cold feeling settled in the pit of my stomach. Did I want to help him, the destroyer of my life? Why should I? And could I? Why should I sacrifice the life I'd built with Ruth to help someone who had done me such a dirty? I looked into Maggie's fear-filled eyes and knew that I would do what I could, not to help him, but to help her, no matter what it cost me.

'Okay,' I said. 'Leave it to me.'

Ruth's troubled eyes met mine over Maggie's bent head. I ignored the questions she so rightfully posed.

And so that night I drove Roger to an outlying airfield where we broke the lock on a hangar door and wheeled a light aircraft out onto the grass strip. In the dark of that cold and windy night, I helped him fuel it and secrete his last precious cargo of emeralds – and then, leaving me to clean up the mess, he taxied down the runway and flew off into the night.

In the meantime, in case his mission was unsuccessful, Maggie had left by car to cross the border to our south. Roger's flight, while necessary if he was avoid time in an African jail, was both dangerous and risky. He would have to keep under the radar and arrive illegally in a new country. Questions were bound to be asked. For the next few weeks Ruth and I waited with trepidation to find out if they'd both made it.

During that phase I was called in for questioning – somehow my role in Roger's disappearance had leaked – and I was lucky not to endure a spell in jail myself. My pulse quickened now as I thought of those times. I had risked all then – and for what? We did eventually get word that Maggie and Roger had arrived safely, not from them, but from others who knew we knew them, and, true to form, they were living the high life, with seemingly not a care in the world.

'You're not listening to me.' Ruth's words brought me back to the present.

I composed my features to erase the bitter wry smile that had settled there.

Ruth shook her head at me. 'Des, don't let them get to you. It's over. We live in a different country now. What they did is all in the past. Don't let them control your life this way. You, we deserve better. If they end up living here near us, so be it. They can't harm us now unless we let them.' Ruth's face was close to mine as she leant over my chair and kissed me on the lips. She tasted of cinnamon and other warm spices.

Then she straightened and turned away from me, and as she did so I realised the truth of her words. I had wasted too much time worrying about Maggie and Roger and their nefarious deeds. I had a new life in a new country, a beautiful wife, three gorgeous kids and five wonderful grandkids, and my wife, while she may not be petite like Maggie, was nevertheless beautiful and majestic. And even though her flaming red hair had morphed to a distinguished silver-grey, her distinctive amber eyes still flashed fire and her creamy olive skin always looked good in her favourite colour: green.

I realised then with certainty that while green might be the colour of Maggie's temptress eyes, and the colour of emeralds and even of jealousy, it was also, for me, the colour of love.

The Message

I stood inside the walk-in robe and examined my clothes. What should I wear? The weather forecast had said it would be twenty-three degrees, so should I wear jeans, or go with a more formal look, perhaps white pants and a black top, or even my new red dress? I chose the jeans and paired them with a flowing green top. Then I took extra care with my make-up and hair, smiling at myself in the mirror. I was behaving like a teenage girl about to go on a date, not a mature sixty-something woman.

How long had it been since our last meeting? Forty years? We'd both been twenty-five then and old beyond our years.

With a last look at myself in the mirror, I went through to the kitchen and picked up my car keys. Was this a mistake? What would my brother John have thought of this, or my late husband Kev, or, for that matter, Rob's late wife Tina? Inhaling deeply, I strode down the passage. If I didn't go I would always wonder. Better to get it over with.

As I drove off, I reflected on the intervening years. We'd first met in 1969 when we both enrolled at the same university, down at the sea, what seemed a million miles away from our troubled and turbulent landlocked home country that had been in the throes of a 'bush' war since 1964. Despite the hardships our country faced, we were so filled with optimism, for ourselves, for our future.

I think I loved Rob from the first minute I saw him. He had that shy smile and solemn yet mocking eyes that seemed to consider each word that was uttered. And he was fun. Those were carefree times, perhaps made more poignant by the memories of what those we had left back home were enduring. We drank too much and went to the formal balls together. We let our hair down at wine and cheese beach parties where the cold sand seeped through fingers and toes and the sea thundered in time with our pulses as we touched and kissed and loved. Sometimes we skipped lectures to spend a morning on the beach, learning to surf.

Despite the wagging, we worked hard.

After four years of study, we both graduated, now two mature adults of twenty-two, but even though we could have gone anywhere in the world, the unspoken message was there: Now we were qualified, we would return to the country of our birth, where we would give back to the society that had raised us, me to teaching and him, although an engineer, conscripted into our army.

I can still remember seeing him standing there in his camouflage gear, hat at a rakish angle, dark hair that had always been worn long and shaggy now cropped close to his head, the cobalt eyes holding a mixture of amusement and concern for what lay ahead. I can also clearly remember how happy I was that Rob, my boyfriend, would be in the same 'stick' as my older brother John. It seemed fitting somehow. I knew they would care for one another. John was two years older than I was and at twenty-four was a veteran of many campaigns. If anyone knew what was going on and how to stay alive, it was him.

'Look after each other,' I said, and kissed Rob.

His lips were soft and cool and tasted of peppermint. I relished the taste of him as I drove on to the school where I would be working, relieved that John and Rob would have each other's backs.

As soon as I rounded the bend, reality set in. I knew this school – I'd been here as a girl – but the sight of the high perimeter fences and the razor wire brought me up short. Even though I was well aware of the true situation, somehow, during my four years away, I hadn't related the way we'd come to live, armed and with security fences, with how it would affect the small children. Would our enemies really attack them? Were they truly that barbaric?

Brought back to the present by the sight of the Glasshouse Mountains to my left as I travelled, I couldn't help but contrast that almost forgotten life with the one I now lived. Even though I was alone after Kev's death four years earlier, my children and grandchildren lived close by, and we all lived a life of peace and tranquillity in our new land.

In that previous life, in the helter-skelter of life as a new teacher, thoughts of Rob retreated into a joyous container, something I would open and bask in at the end of each hectic day. Memories of him and his strong arms and masculine scent made my senses sing, and I longed for him with every part of my being.

And so it was with shock that I received that terrible message: John had been badly injured in a terrorist encounter, and Rob was to blame.

By the time I reached the hospital, my folks were already there. I walked in, feeling hollow inside, and scarcely recognised the bloodied and broken figure lying on the bed. His head was bandaged and one eye swollen shut, his face so grotesquely swollen that his features were distorted. But it was his legs that had taken the brunt.

'They'll have to amputate them.' My dad's voice sounded hoarse. He and John had always been close. 'It seems he's lost the use of his arms too. There's shrapnel embedded in his spine.'

As the enormity of what had befallen John sank in, I wondered what lay in store for him. He had always been such a vibrant, live-life-at-full-steam type of person. How would he cope as a quadriplegic?

Feeling sick to my stomach, I went in search of Rob and found him, alone and brooding, on the banks of the slow-moving river. He was different, distant, with a reserve I couldn't comprehend.

'Why?' I asked him, my hand seeking to burrow itself in his. 'What happened out there?' I held my breath, half afraid he would tell me.

Beyond us, the waters of the river sparkled and a fish eagle screeched overhead.

But he, of the considered opinions, at first had no words to express how he felt. Then the torrent began to flow. Their 'stick' had been shot at by helicopters from our own army, who had mistaken them for a band of armed terrorists. They fled, seeking cover from those clattering impersonal birds shooting spurts of iron fire from their bellies, and then, the next day, they had come across a small boy in the veld.

'I should have shot him.'

My lip trembled. 'Shot who?'

'I was closest and I had him in my sights. All I had to do was squeeze the trigger. I should have done it. But he was running away, like a scared rabbit, his big tatty coat flapping like ragged wings.

'John urged: "Do it!" But I let him go.

'"He'll warn the terrs, man," John said. "They'll be on us like flies on carrion. We'd better get out of here chop-chop."

'I didn't want to believe it. But he was right. We hadn't gone five hundred metres and they were waiting for us. They cut John and two others down

77

in the first round. The rest of us ducked for cover and returned fire. It was mayhem, man, complete mayhem.'

From the haunted look in his eyes I could sense what they had gone through. It was almost as if I could hear the rat-tat-tat of the AK-47s, hear the thump and whistle as the bullets ploughed through trees and thwanged off into the veld. There would have been screaming and yelling and bloodcurdling curses – and then the silence, worse than any deafening noise could have been. As if the world was waiting, catching its breath, watching to see what new agony would come next.

'How old was he?'

'Tiny ... five, six years old.'

I thought of the little ones I had been teaching, their innocent faces and sweet smiles. I remembered my thoughts when I'd first seen the razor wire.

As I gazed at Rob sitting there, lobbing flat stones into the water, his cheeks scratched from thorns, body cut and bruised, I reflected on how my brother would never walk again, and might not even live. And yet here was Rob, who I had relied on, and he had survived almost unscathed. When I gazed into his eyes I knew he read my silent message as undeniably as if I had spoken it out loud. No words to the contrary would convince him. I saw him crumple then fill with resolve. He would survive, with or without me, and I knew then it would be without me.

My heart thumped as I took the off-ramp and negotiated the turns to the Caboolture Historical Village. In his message, Rob had suggested we meet there and I'd agreed – it was an significant attraction and easy to find, and we both had a strong interest in the past. Besides, it would give us something to look at and discuss should our meeting prove awkward. A coffee shop would be too intimate; there wouldn't be the same distractions. It was fitting too: a historical village as a meeting place for two people with a long and tortured history.

His message had said: Meet me at the Post Office.

I parked the car and looked around. Yes, there it was. With some trepidation, I walked towards the small old-fashioned building. I couldn't see him there. Perhaps he'd changed his mind. A flutter of disappointment passed through me, and suddenly I realised how much I wanted to see him.

As my shoes crunched across a patch of gravel, I spied someone standing to one side of the building, inspecting its architecture, hands in the pockets of his jeans, his back to me. I hesitated. Was that him? He had broad shoulders like Rob, although slightly stooped, but the hair, rather than dark brown, was thinning and grey. Yet when he turned, I saw that the eyes still burned with that same intense sapphire, and his smile, lopsided and sardonic, was identical.

I went forward, hand outstretched in a formal greeting. Rob ignored the gesture and scooped me into a bear-hug instead. He smelt of soap and a fresh spicy aftershave, and I relished the warmth of his body so close to mine.

'It's good to see you,' he said. 'You look just like you did forty years ago; I'd have recognised you anywhere.'

I knew it was a lie, but I enjoyed the compliment anyway; I knew it was well meant.

'You look great too,' I said, and he did.

'Shall we go inside?' He gestured towards the Post Office door.

I preceded him into the building with its old smells and history, and we spent the next two hours wandering the village, absorbing times gone by while we talked of our past.

When the time came to leave, I stood in the car park, holding his hands in mine, and the inevitable question came to my mind: Would we be able to forge a new relationship, or would our past always contaminate our present? As I looked into his eyes I knew the answer: Yes. We had both moved on from the trauma we'd experienced, we'd both suffered and loved and borne children. We'd both loved and lost our life partners, but we had also learnt much in the intervening years, and there was enough left between

81

us that we could write a new history together. We could take it slowly and see where events took us. And, no matter what transpired between us, we could look forward to a fine future, together or apart. That message was loud and clear.

Eh?

Rosie looked across at the elderly man sitting opposite her. Grey hair, neatly trimmed; eyes the colour of sapphires. Fit looking, as though he worked out most days. She focused on his hands: long elegant fingers ending in clean manicured nails.

But his job, his profession when he was younger, it seemed so obscure. What on earth would a navel plucker actually do? She'd heard of lint in people's navels. Is that what he did: plucked lint from people's bellies, sort of like a masseuse or some kind of alternative practitioner; or had he tended to people who worshipped Buddha; or perhaps made sure the navels of newborn babies didn't become inverted?

Who knew?

He sipped on his white wine and then looked her way. She crinkled her eyes at him and bared her teeth in a grin. He resumed his conversation with the man on his right.

Then again, perhaps she'd misheard. He might have said 'naval plucker', in which case he could have been one of those navy rescue men who leapt out of helicopters and plucked drowning victims from storm-tossed waves.

She examined him again.

Yes, she decided, he was the hero type. She could see him dangling from a winch cable above a stormy sea, the sound of the rotors whipping away his shouted instructions as he grappled to rescue yet another unfortunate.

Her heart beat faster.

She placed the last of her smoked salmon into her mouth and delicately chewed it. She noted his well-cut clothes, his poise and the ease with which he carried on a conversation.

Dabbing her mouth with her serviette, she leaned forward and patted his hand with her fingers.

'Peter dear, do tell me exactly what a naval plucker does. It sounds ever so exciting.'

Peter's eyes opened wider. 'Not a naval plucker, Rosie: travel doctor. I think you misunderstood me.'

END

About the Author

Kathy Stewart was born in South Africa, and she and her husband now live on the Gold Coast, Australia.

Other books by the same author are:

Chameleon

Mark of the Leopard

Self-Editing Your Novel

Writing Memoirs

Star Turn and Other Stories

Over to You

The Armoured Train Incident

Betty Bee's Garden Adventure (as Kathleen Stewart)

Chelsea and the Chestnut Charger

If you enjoyed this book, please consider leaving a review on Goodreads or the site where you bought it. Reviews are so important to independent authors. Thanks!

Contact Kathy at Kathystewart640@gmail.com or check out her web site: http://www.authorsally.net

Excerpt from:

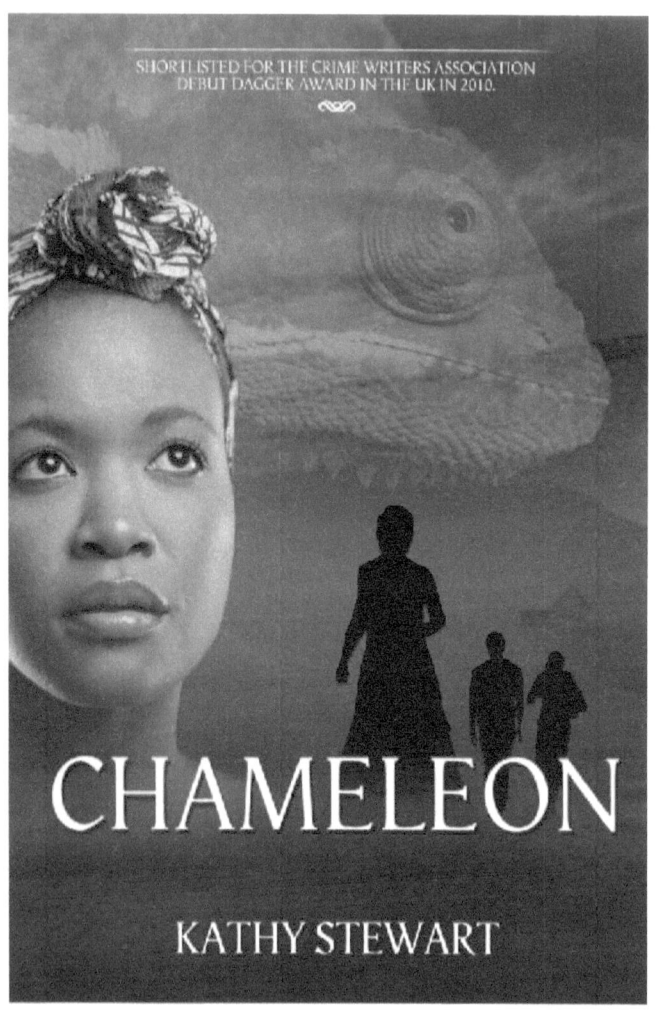

SHORTLISTED FOR THE CRIME WRITERS ASSOCIATION
DEBUT DAGGER AWARD IN THE UK IN 2010.

CHAMELEON

KATHY STEWART

Chapter 1

Transkei, South Africa

19th October, 1914

Mandla stumbled to his knees, gasping for breath, and dropped his spear and the bundle onto the veld. The air rasped his throat; his thighs burned from running. Spikes of grass dug into his knees. Then the cold fingers of fear gripped his gut, forcing him to his feet again. With trembling hands, he picked up his spear and the parcel, and staggered on, his young body now weak with fatigue; naked, exposed on the open veld for all to see. The bundle weighed heavy on his arm, scratching his bare skin where it rubbed against his side.

When he reached the smooth boulders at the river's edge, he flung the package out as far as he could. It bobbed a while on the current, then floated downstream. He watched until it disappeared from sight, willing it to the River Spirits who live on the dry land beneath the surface.

Soil and congealed blood coated the tip of his spear. He dipped the blade into the swirling water and watched the water strip the soil away, followed by the black blood – it turned red, then pink, as it flowed from the tip. He scrubbed at the blade, the blood slippery beneath his fingers. He wanted to recoil but made himself persist until the spear seemed clean again beneath the clear water. But it would never be the same; nothing would ever be the same.

He hurled it with all his force out over the water. It spiralled through the air then landed with a clatter on the rocks, before bouncing into the water and floating off. When it had gone, he waded out, the current tugging at his shins.

He dipped his hands in, feeling the coldness against his skin, watching as the blood floated free, and waited for the release the water would bring. But it wasn't enough. He picked up handfuls of coarse gravel from the riverbed and scrubbed at his hands until the palms bled and his blood stained the water.

Through the ripples distorting his reflection, his face looked wrinkled and sad, mouth drooping, more like that of a spent old man rather than a warrior nearing his prime.

He turned his palms up to examine them. Pink, criss-crossed with fine lines where the stones had cut gouges, and chafed raw – yet still they felt tainted. He waded out further and splashed water onto his arms and legs, rubbing at the flesh.

Thunder rumbled behind him. He glanced over his shoulder. Clouds had gathered over Thab'nyama's jagged peaks, shrouding the summit and lending an eerie light to the veld. The greens seemed to shine from within, as if a fire had been lit inside each blade. Once the rain came, the swiftly flowing water would purge the thing from his life forever.

From this distance, the cave entrance looked like a tiny speck on Thab'nyama's face, so small that no one would find it if they didn't already know where to look.

He shivered in the stiff breeze coming off the storm, then followed the path twisting beside the river towards the kraal he shared with his family. Thorny brush snatched at his ankles, but the pain was welcome. He walked on, allowing the blood to flow down onto his feet unhindered. It snaked in scarlet rivulets to his calloused soles, where it mingled with the baked-earth hardness of the path.

A cracking flash of lightning ripped across the sky, followed by a loud clap of thunder that jolted his thoughts. Heavy drops began to fall, splattering onto the parched earth, gaining in intensity until the smooth surface of the track became slick and he slithered with each step.

A thin trail of smoke writhing into the air heralded the kraal. He negotiated the hill, past the flock of goats scavenging on the sparse grass, to where the thatched roofs pointed skyward.

Chickens huddled near the door to the cooking hut, finding shelter from the rain under the shallow eaves. He shooed them away and they ran through the curtain of raindrops cascading off the roof. Squawking, they held their bodies upright, wings pressed close to their sides.

He ducked in through the entrance. The heat inside was stifling.

'*Hau*, I thought the lightning had got you,' his mother commented.

She sat near the fire, her wrinkled face upturned, body shrivelled, as if dried out in the dull glow from the embers, the ochre cloth of her skirt hiding her stick-like legs. The bangles on her bare arms accentuated their thinness. Behind her, on shelves fashioned by Mandla's father, stood gourds of all sizes, and pots turned with her own hands, baked

93

with care in the kiln she had built behind the cluster of huts.

He knew she was only half joking. She held a stick in her hands, her eyes enquiring as she surveyed his naked body glistening in the firelight.

'Where are your clothes?'

'They were wet. I took them off outside,' he lied.

'You have hurt yourself.'

Water dripped onto his hand as he touched his bruised cheek. The swelling must be more noticeable than he'd thought.

'I fell.'

It came out sharper than he'd intended.

Nontle's eyes registered resentment. She turned towards the fire, poking at the glowing embers with the well-worn stick.

Mandla rolled some *dagga* and lit it. Inhaling deeply, he waited for it to bring peace from the haunting images of the Chameleon that threatened to engulf him. The sound of the rain beating on the earth outside dulled his senses. He lay down on a mat and closed his eyes, hoping that the demons

94

would be flushed away by the river and the welcome rain...

***

Chameleon is available at most online bookstores.

Contact Kathy at

Kathystewart640@gmail.com or check out her web site

http://www.authorsally.net

Excerpt from:

The Armoured Train Incident

KATHY STEWART

The Armoured Train Incident

Wednesday, 15th November, 1899

Senior Combat General Louis Botha stood up in his stirrups and peered into the thick mist blanketing the veld. His horse shifted beneath him and tugged at the reins held loosely in his hands. The sound was unmistakeable. Then the trail of smoke barrelling into the air told him he was right. The shape rumbling out of the white swirls, puffing black breaths into the leaden skies, gradually solidified.

97

This was indeed most fortunate. When Botha and his patrol had set off that morning, their expedition was only meant to be for reconnaissance, to see if and when they could attack Estcourt. And then this – the armoured train huffing importantly towards them through the sodden early morning air, the light still grey with the sun barely peeping over the horizon. The train rattled over the trestle bridge spanning the Blaauw Krantz River, heading north.

The burghers waited behind the shelter afforded by the hills overlooking the railway line and watched as the train chugged slowly past. Close-up – so close they could smell the soot and glimpse the faces of the men inside the armoured carriages – the noise of the train seemed hesitant, each halting puff like the expelling of a held-in breath as the train ground past them on its way to Chieveley.

When it had gone, the Boers rolled boulders onto the tracks, grunting with the effort. Then they stood back and grinned, slapping each other on the back as they surveyed their handiwork. Botha deployed three field guns and a quick-firing Maxim on the hill above the track. Now all they had to do was wait.

Aboard the train, the stoker, Alexander Stewart, worked away steadily, shovelling coal into the massive furnace to keep the steam up. It was hard, hot work and he was covered in black dust, but he was used to it. Although a qualified driver, he often doubled as a fireman. This day, an older man, Charlie Wagner, was in charge. They'd set off from Estcourt, nearly twenty miles down the line, heading for Frere and thence via Chieveley to Colenso, the fifth such trip in ten days.

'Be careful to keep out of reach of the Boer guns,' Colonel Long, the garrison commander at Estcourt, had cautioned as he handed Captain Aylmer Haldane, the leader of the expedition, his instructions.

A curious order from an artillery man, thought Alex. Surely he of all people would know field guns could be moved anywhere at will, while the train was limited to the tracks?

'We must make use of these modern contraptions,' Long was fond of saying, but the men knew, despite its armour, the train was an ambush

99

waiting to happen. 'Wilson's death trap,' the men called it, though who Wilson was had long been swallowed in the mists of time.

***

The Armoured Train Incident is available at most online bookstores.

Contact Kathy at

Kathystewart640@gmail.com or check out her web site

http://www.authorsally.net

Excerpt from:

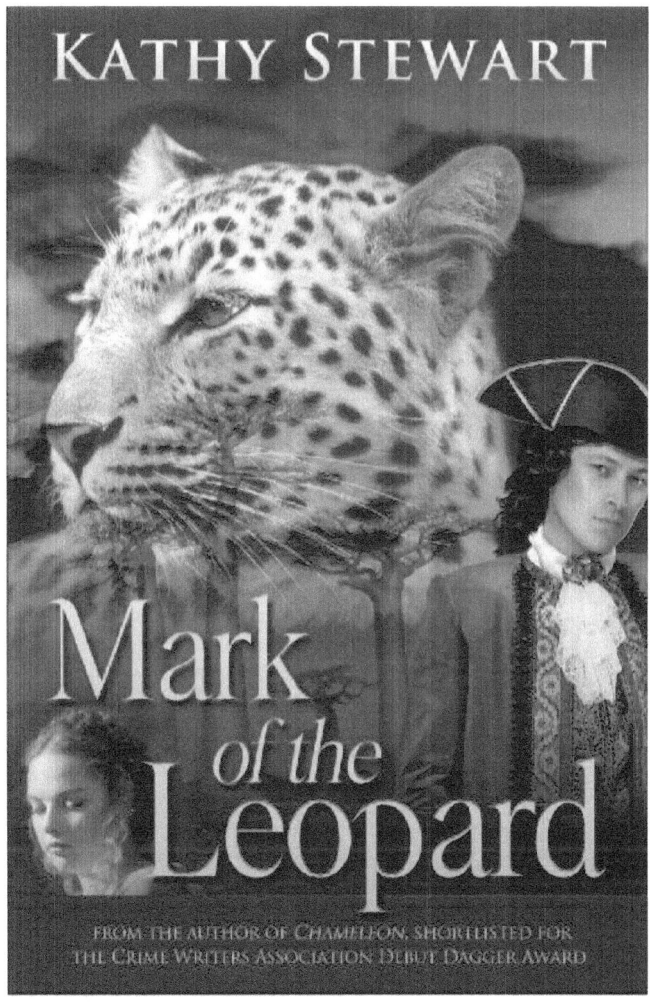

KATHY STEWART

Mark *of the* Leopard

FROM THE AUTHOR OF *CHAMELEON*, SHORTLISTED FOR
THE CRIME WRITERS ASSOCIATION DEBUT DAGGER AWARD

Chapter 1

1703

Madagascar Island

Tom lay against the sailor's tunic, too tired to speak as the tar plucked him from the pallet and carried him out of the dank cabin to where the boat lay bobbing in the water. He could see it, far below the ship's sides. His mam was beside him, her face all twisted with worry. She clasped the pendant his da' had given her and turned it first this way then that.

The sailor held him tightly as he launched himself over the edge, clutching onto him with one hand and onto the slippery wet rope with the other. Nimble as a temple monkey, he swung down the rungs to the boat waiting below. Tom could see first water then sky, water then sky, water then sky and his head reeled.

He tried to cry out, but it came as a dry croak, muffled against the coarse cloth. When he looked up, there was his mam, her tiny figure cloaked in a big dress, coming hand over hand down the rope ladder after them as she clung on to the rough rope for dear life.

Beyond her, leaning over the ship's rail, Tom could see Nanny's face, all puckered, and below, hands gripping the rail, was little Sarah, her long black hair whipping in the wind, small face pinched closed with the worry. Conway, who was still only five, leant his head against Nanny and buried his cheek into her garments. He looked upon Tom solemnly as he was borne further from their view.

The sailor laid Tom down on the bare planks and picked up the oars. Another man held his hands out for his mam and helped her into the boat, which rocked alarmingly and bumped against the huge

103

wooden side of the vessel. The oarsman cursed under his breath, but they had been subjected to far worse in the weeks since leaving India. The men's faces were grim as they pushed the boat clear of the bigger vessel and started the long pull for shore.

His mam sat beside Tom and laid her hand upon his brow.

'Why aren't Conway and Sarah coming too?' he managed to croak out. 'Doesn't Grandfather want to see them?' Talking made him hot and he thrashed about, wanting to be free of the cloying heat, the suffocation that threatened to choke him.

'Be still, Tom,' his mam said. 'We'll be there soon.'

The only other sound was the slap of the waves on the hull and the grunts of the tars pulling on the oars.

'Nearly there.'

His mam's urgent words penetrated the fog that clouded Tom's mind. He raised his head. There, in the distance but growing bigger with each stroke, lay some crude huts grouped along the shoreline. Smoke

104

rose in tendrils from their thatched roofs. It didn't look anything like he could remember from when they'd left England with his da', and Grandfather had been so angry with him – with all of them. He could still remember his grandfather's fierce red-veined eyes, the way he glowered at them and shouted. But that was four years ago now, when Tom was just a little lad, Conway's age, and his da' was still with them then.

As they drew nearer, Tom could hear the gentle pluff of the waves breaking on the shore, the shouts of men gathered there. The boat's hull scraped against sand. The sailor lifted him from the boards and held him at arm's length as he stepped into the shallow water. He waded onto the beach, and some men came forward.

'Stay back.' He broke into a pidgin language and they obeyed, their eyes round and fearful.

They were savages, barely dressed, except for a cloth tied about their loins. Their skin was dark and their black hair straight as Tom's.

105

'Is this England? Is Grandfather here?' Tom managed to gasp out, but his mam shook her head, and Tom looked around at the strange people and their strange houses, wondering why they were here.

The tar carrying Tom stopped before an impressive hut, larger than the rest. He laid him upon the ground under the shade of a swaying palm and walked off, brushing the boy's fever from his sleeves and chest. Sabrina sat beside her son, her hand resting lightly upon his shoulder, then upon his brow.

They waited there a while. Smoke was all about, and Tom could smell the salt air, the fish the men had recently caught, the tang of crushed plants. And above him the palm leaves rustled and swayed in the breeze coming off the sea.

At last came a messenger, and at his instruction the sailor lifted Tom and carried him further along the beach, the boy's body jiggling in his arms as he walked. Tom groaned as he fought nausea, and closed his eyes.

Then they were inside a hut and Sabrina's worried face was peering down at him. She wiped his brow with her hand and it felt cool, blessedly cool. He fell into a troubled sleep, where he dreamt that he was abandoned there on that island with these strange people and he could not tell them who he was or what he wanted.

When he regained consciousness, his mam was still at his side. He reached out his hand to touch her. She would care for him, until he was well and strong again and they could continue their journey to meet up with his grandfather, Mr Barrington.

But Sabrina was not smiling. The tears were still there, her cheeks glinting in the half-light. She took the pendant from her chain and held it out to a wrinkled crone kneeling in the gloom beside her near Tom's feet.

'Use this.' She handed the pendant to the woman. 'Make it the same.'

Tom watched, puzzled, as the old lady took the pendant from his mam, then uncovered his foot and laid her other hand upon it. Her grip was firm, and she held his ankle like a vice. At a gesture from her, Sabrina grasped Tom's shin in her tiny hand, not looking at his face. Then from the open box beside her, the old crone selected a needle and inks and began to carve the image on the pendant onto the tender sole of his foot, mumbling, her withered gums working as she laboured.

He writhed and cried out, begging his mam to make it stop, but she only gripped him tighter, not speaking, tears running down her cheek into the corner of her mouth.

When the old woman had finished, she leant back on her haunches and examined her handiwork by the light of a smoky torch. His foot stung where she had cut into him. The orange flame guttered in the breeze coming through the door. Sabrina unclasped a brooch from her blouse and held it out to the woman. The old hag's hand closed over the pendant and Sabrina's eyes went wide.

'No,' she cried. 'Not that. Take this. I beg you.'

But the old hag held fast and Sabrina stood in the low hut, her back bumping against the roof before

108

she managed to wrest the pendant from the old crone's hand. She reattached it to the chain around her neck and let it slide down into the valley between her breasts. The woman left, ducking out through the doorway and they could hear her muttering in her mad low cackle as she limped away across the clearing.

'We have to go.' The sailor who had carried Tom was at the hut door, standing well back so he would not breathe in the boy's fever-laden air. His voice was urgent and gruff above the sound of the waves. There was a deathly hush, as if the world was holding its breath, and Tom heard his mam weeping softly.

'Are we going now?' He was suddenly filled with dread. The thought of the journey back to the ship in that tiny boat was more than he could bear.

Sabrina's mouth puckered and tears tracked through the sweat-sheen on her cheeks. She shook her head and moved towards the doorway, her silhouette blocking the light.

'Mam,' Tom cried out. 'Where are you going?'

But she was already outside and he could hear her words, spoken with haste and some urgency to the crewman who now waited out of the boy's sight.

'Please, he's my son; he's only nine. Give me time.'

'We have no time,' said the crewman. 'The tide be right now. The captain told you afor'un we left the ship. We sail, with or without you. It's your choice, but the boy stays.'

The words slammed into Tom. He struggled to sit up, but the sickness overwhelmed him. When he opened his eyes, his mam was beside him. He stretched out a hand to touch her, and she knelt down beside him and gazed deep into his eyes. She forced words through parched lips. Tears streamed down her face.

'I'll be back. Somehow, I will find you again.'

Then she ducked out through the entrance to the hut and was joined by the sailors. Together they walked off towards a banana grove and the path that led to the beach. Tom stretched out a feeble hand for her, but no cry would come and he was too dry for tears. His body burned with the fever and his eyes could only take in the shimmering shapes as they disappeared from his view.

Chapter 2

1703

Cape of Good Hope

The wind howled through the rigging, tearing at the tattered remnants of the sails. Icy water broke over the deck in a foaming rage. The *Swan* was being wrenched apart by massive seas, her timbers creaking and groaning as each successive wave pounded her cracked timbers.

'Oh, dear Lord, please help us.' Sabrina was on deck, her entreaty torn from her lips as she struggled to maintain her balance and her grip on Nanny and the children as the water tore past over the ship's bow, threatening to drag them into the sea.

Water streamed down Sabrina's face, plastering her long black hair to her cheeks, her clothes soaked through, moulded to her body. All around, men in sodden tunics manoeuvred back and forth, going hand over hand along ropes, shouting to each other, their words whipped away by the gale-force wind as they strove to lower the boats.

A mast smashed through the starboard rail. The boiling sea raged up through the rent timbers, pushing Sabrina towards the rails then sucking her back towards the gaping holes. She clung onto the children and Nanny, afraid they would be plucked from her grasp, and looked into their terrified eyes, wondering if this would be the last time she would see them. No. That couldn't be. She had to save them. But how? And what of Tom? If they perished now, he would think she had abandoned him forever. The ache and betrayal she knew he had felt at her leaving him would be cast in his mind for eternity. There would be no time for amends.

Struggling to keep her balance on the pitching timbers, Sabrina took a deep breath and released her hold on Nanny and the children. With cold-numbed hands, she began to tear strips from her dress. Bracing herself on unsteady legs, she passed the first strip through the children's belts and then fastened it to her waist, resisting as she again threatened to slither towards the shattered rail.

She tore another strip from her gown and reached out for Nanny.

Their wet hands touched.

But then a wall of green water reared above their heads, dwarfing them. Sabrina cried out. Sarah and Conway shrieked as the wave broke, rushing down like an avalanche to sweep their legs from under them and sluice their harnessed bodies over the side in a tumbling heap of arms and legs. Nanny was torn from Sabrina's grasp, and the last Sabrina saw of her was her screaming mouth and wide-open eyes before she was swallowed by the sea.

Down and down they went, twisting and turning over and over, debris tearing at their flesh. Sabrina's chest burned for air, but she held on, pressing her mouth tight closed, flailing desperately for Conway and Sarah, afraid they would be swept from her. She could feel the tug of their weight on her waist, but all she could see was the churning white foam and sea-green water. The children and her long dress were weighing her down.

With all her will, she forced herself to keep in the air that tortured her lungs. With consciousness slowly ebbing, she kicked out with all her might, using her arms to pull at the water as she strove to find air for herself and her children ...

Contact Kathy at

Kathystewart640@gmail.com or check out her web site

http://www.authorsally.net